Printed in the United States of America.   ISBN 0-8167-4926-4

10 9 8 7 6 5 4 3 2

Valentine's Day is coming!
We will have a party at school.

Dad and I make cards.

Mom and I bake cupcakes.

It's Valentine's Day! We have a party at school.

We get cards. We have cupcakes.

It's time to go home.

"Hi, Mom! Look at all my Valentine cards!"

Look! What is this?

It's a puppy.
A Valentine puppy!

What a cute puppy!

But whose puppy is it?

Does the puppy have a home?

Miss Cook looks for a collar.

The puppy has no collar.

I love the Valentine puppy.

"Mom, can we bring the puppy home?"

"Yes, we can bring the puppy home."

The puppy loves the car!

We give the puppy a drink.

What a mess!

We give the puppy a bath.

The puppy loves the bath!

Dad comes home.

"Look, Dad—a puppy!
Can we keep the puppy?"

"Yes, we can keep the puppy."

"Forever?"

"Yes, forever."

I love my Valentine puppy. Forever.